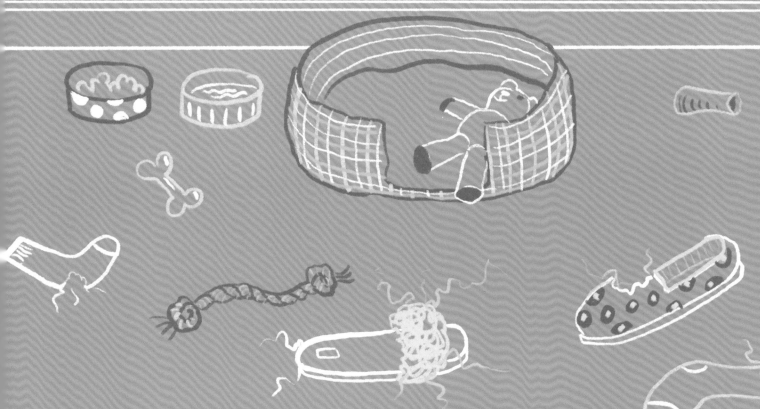

For Lizzy, who inspires me with her kindness and wonderful gift caring for dogs - CG

For Mika, my foot warming pal - UH

ROO and SARGE

to the rescue

It was a gloomy, grey day and Roo the Cockapoo was looking out of her kennel window waiting for visitors at Springfield Dogs Home, where she had been living for a few years.

Roo had been brought into the home because her owner could no longer look after her. She had lost her eye some years ago, so had to wear a patch for protection.

Roo had many friends at Springfield. She had seen lots of lonely dogs arrive and then leave with tails wagging when a new family adopted them. She always felt very sad that nobody wanted to take her home. She knew it was because she had a patch on her eye.

Her best friend was a retired police dog, Sarge the German Shepherd, who used to help his detective owner with his police work. Sarge had done some amazing things helping to keep people safe. He had lost one of his legs in the line of duty, so had, had to retire.

Sarge always reassured Roo that one day they would both be chosen to go home with a new owner, who would appreciate their company. Their kennels were next to one another.

"Come on Sarge and Roo, time for some fresh air," shouted Mr Croshaw, who owned the home for dogs.

Sarge could still walk and run, even though he only had three legs, and Roo could see very well, even though she only had one eye.

"Come on, Roo! I'll race you on the field," barked
Sarge, as their kennel doors opened.
"Ok," woofed Roo.
Off they ran.

The dogs home had a huge field, so that they could get as much fresh air and exercise as possible, and mix with their friends to play and chat.

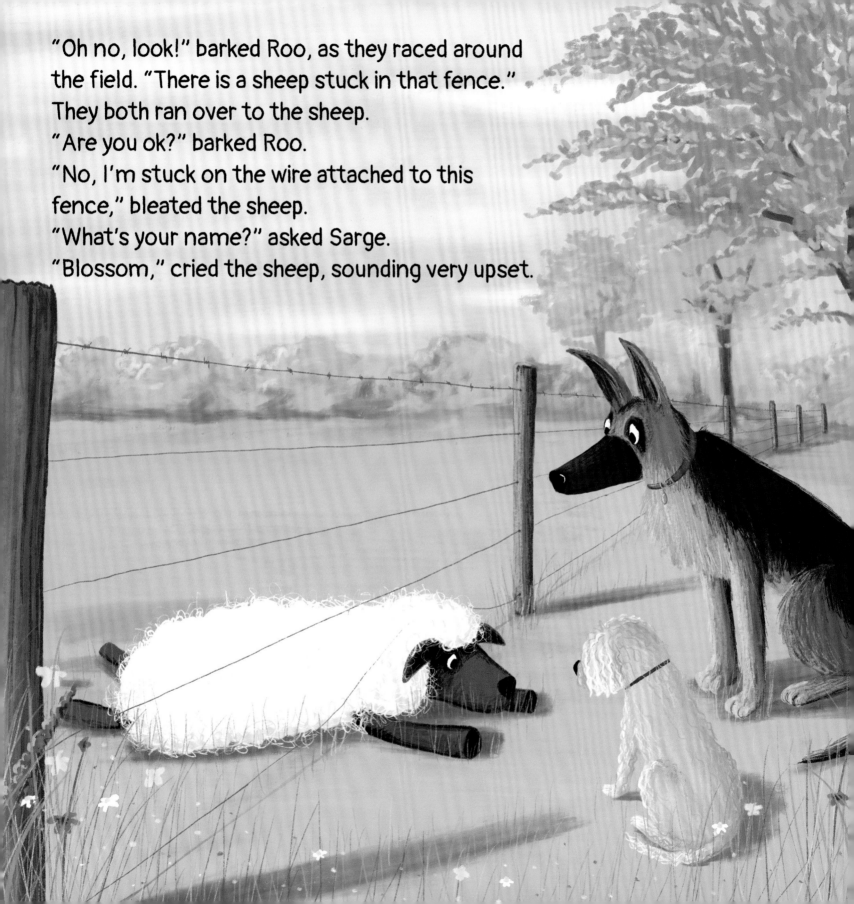

"Oh no, look!" barked Roo, as they raced around the field. "There is a sheep stuck in that fence." They both ran over to the sheep.

"Are you ok?" barked Roo.

"No, I'm stuck on the wire attached to this fence," bleated the sheep.

"What's your name?" asked Sarge.

"Blossom," cried the sheep, sounding very upset.

"We'll get help," replied Sarge, thinking of his police training.
"I'll stay with you," barked Roo. "Sarge will go for help."

Sarge ran back towards the home and barked to get the attention of the owner, Mr Croshaw

"What's wrong, Sarge?" asked Mr Croshaw puzzled.
Sarge continued to bark loudly. Mr Croshaw knew Sarge well
enough to know that something was wrong.
"What is it boy?"

Sarge started running towards the exercise field and Mr Croshaw followed. They could now see Roo with Blossom the sheep.

As they reached the fence, Mr Croshaw
shouted, "Oh dear, we must get help from the
farmer."
Blossom let out a loud baa and tried to
struggle free of the wire.
"Don't worry," Mr Croshaw said, stroking her
head. "We will help you."

Mr Croshaw had been showing some visitors around, who were now looking on with great interest. They were hoping to adopt a dog from the home.

Mr and Mrs Battersea, with their daughter Ruby, who had also been adopted from the age of two, had come to choose a dog.

"Look at those two dogs there, Ruby, aren't they wonderful! They have helped bring attention to that poor sheep who is stuck in the fence," said Mrs Battersea.

Mr Croshaw contacted the farmer, who arrived at the fence from the opposite side.

"Oh dear, Blossom! We will cut you free, don't worry," Farmer Todd reassured the worried sheep.

Sarge, Roo, Mr Croshaw, Mr and Mrs Battersea, and Ruby looked on with great delight, as Farmer Todd cut Blossom the sheep free.
"Hoorah! Well done Roo and Sarge," they all chorused.

"What wonderful dogs you are Roo and Sarge," said Mr Battersea.

"They're fantastic! Can we adopt Roo and Sarge, and take them both home with us?" pleaded Ruby.

Mr and Mrs Battersea looked at one another.
Roo and Sarge looked at one another too with huge smiles of hope on their faces, wagging their tails.
Mr and Mrs Battersea could not refuse. They both replied, "Yes, they are both perfect."

Roo the Cockapoo and Sarge the German Shepherd were so excited that someone finally wanted to take them to a new home.

Author: Christina Gabbitas
Illustrator: Ursula Hurst

First edition 2022

A catalogue record of this book is available in the British Library.
ISBN: 9781739835576
Printed and bound in the UK by Wood Richardson, York.
All papers used by Poems & Pictures Publishing are natural, recyclable products. The manufacturing processes conform to the environmental regulations of the country of origin.

Special thanks to Rebecca Thomas, editor.
To find out more about our team and books visit www.poemsandpicturespublishing.org

Author
Christina Gabbitas
www.christinagabbitas.com

Illustrator
Ursula Hurst
www.artdaze.co.uk